Praise for Star Shapes

"Star Shapes is a propulsive novella—the mystery at the heart of it drove me to finish it in one sitting. Ivy Grimes is a brilliant writer with a keen understanding of what makes a person fall in love with a story. This is a book with texture, a place that feels lived in and weird. I'd recommend this novella to everyone!"

Brandi Wells, author of *The Cleaner*

"Grimes writes with a beguiling innocence that—like a spider—draws you into its web and holds you there until it has drained all the blood from your body. Star Shapes is no different. A sugar-soaked marvel of a story with one hell of an ending."

Caleb Stephens, author of *The Girls in the Cabin and Feeders*

"In Star Shapes, the talented Ivy Grimes explores questions of identity, justice, and belief with a clear and sharp eye. I found it a wholly unique tale, charming and disquieting at once, grounded in the best of Southern Gothic fiction and yet reaching out towards the stars."

Christi Nogle, author of Bram Stoker Award® winning novel *Beulah*

"A strange, compelling exploration of captivity, justice, complicity, and monstrosity, with a voice that will catch you from the start and an ending that will leave you haunted. Star Shapes is a must-read for fans of psychological horror!"

Kelsea Yu, Shirley Jackson Award-nominated *author of Bound Feet*

"This subtly unnerving story of Southern discomfort is a remarkable chimera of a novella, living in the blurry nexus of memory and identity. Invoking such spirits as Flannery O'Connor and Shirley Jackson—but wholly Ivy Grimes—Star Shapes will haunt your memory long after you have set the book down."

TJ Price, author of *The Disappearance of Tom Nero*

Star Shapes
by Ivy Grimes
with illustrations by Alana Baldwin

Star Shapes. Copyright © 2023 by Ivy Grimes

First Edition

Cover copyright and design, interior formatting © 2023 by Alana Baldwin.

Published by Spooky House Press, LLC.
East Islip, NY, 11730, USA
www.spookyhousepress.com

ISBN: 978-1-959946-14-4 (Paperback)
ISBN: 978-1-959946-15-1 (eBook)

Printed in the United States of America

1.

The little boy wore overalls with no shirt or shoes. He even had a little smudge of dirt on his cheek, and he looked so cute that I wanted to take his picture. He was crying, saying he was all alone in the city because he'd lost his mother. I told him I'd help.

"Where do you think your mom went? Why did she come downtown?" I asked as I walked around with him. I could tell he was probably from somewhere in the country between Birmingham and Selma, or Birmingham and Tuscaloosa. He had a thick little accent, too.

"Going shopping," he said.

"Shopping for what?"

"Furniture. And...tools?"

He took my hand like a little sweetheart, like he was scared. My heart melted towards him even more. I don't spend much time with kids except for my niece, and to be honest, I get tired of her sometimes. But if you're only around kids for a little while, they seem so innocent.

Hardly anyone else was downtown that early. I'd arrived at the office parking lot around six in the morning after my early yoga class, and I figured I'd go on into work so my bosses would be impressed. For my first job out of college, I'd landed an entry-level position in HR at a big law firm. I mostly answered the phone and moved papers around, but the lady who hired me promised she was going to help me rise in the ranks. I didn't have that much work to do that morning, but I knew I could mess around and fill the time until everyone else got there and saw how serious I was.

The little boy found me while I was in the parking lot beside my building. Once he had me by the hand, he led me down a lonely street full of shops that hadn't opened yet. From there, he led me down a narrow alley.

"You think your mom is back here?" I said, figuring he was confused but not wanting to discourage him. There was nothing back there but piles of trash.

Imagine my surprise when two men jumped out from behind a bunch of trash bags. They were wearing ski masks, and their arms were outstretched like they were going to fight me, and I almost died right there.

It was like it was happening to someone else. Men had always tried to help me and protect me, and no one had ever tried to hurt me before. Well, that isn't quite true, but it's almost true. It depends on what you mean by hurt, and as my grandmother always said, no one passes through the river without getting a chill. The main thing is, I'd never been kidnapped before.

They grabbed my purse, which had my phone, and they tied my wrists behind my back, tied my feet together, put me in their trunk. I tried my best to shout, but they put fabric around my mouth before I could really holler out. All I could do was squeak, and I forgot to cry "Help!" or "Fire!" All I could think to say was "Why me?"

God, that car ride was the worst kind of darkness of my life. Millions, maybe billions of thoughts ran through my head as I rode along, bumped around by their shoddy car and reckless driving, I thought I'd die on my way to wherever. And if I survived the ride, were they going to kill me or just hurt me? Was there a heaven and a hell? How would my family take the news? Had the boy gotten away? If he escaped, surely he would tell the police. I was terrified, yes, but never hopeless.

Once the car finally stopped, I rehearsed the speech I was going to make to my kidnappers. I'd offer money and sympathy. I would make them understand how much I wanted to live. I'd cry, and they might feel sorry for me and set me free. Maybe they'd even apologize. You never knew what might happen! They were from the country, after all. Country people are usually so polite.

When the trunk popped open, the two men weren't wearing masks anymore. I could see that one was older, almost middle-aged, and the other was no more than a teenager.

Probably just a high school kid. I wished I'd kicked harder while I had the chance. What surprised me most, though, was that the little boy in overalls stood beside them, with all of them peering in at me like I was a new pet they were bringing home.

I realized that the boy had been the bait. I'd been lured like a fish.

Finally, the man pulled me out of the trunk and put me gently on the grass. He was tall and broad, at least twice my size, so he managed me easily while I was fruitlessly kicking at him. We were in the middle of a stretch of farmland, in the dusty driveway of a decrepit old house that had once been white but now needed a pressure wash and a new coat of paint. Just the kind of place I'd imagined that little overalled boy living.

They untied the cloth from around my mouth, and I spit out some lint and got my breath. I must have been half-suffocated without realizing it.

"Please!" That was the first thing I said. "Please don't hurt me! I promise I won't press charges if you take me back right now. You wouldn't have taken me if you weren't in need, I know. You're good people. My parents have plenty of money, and they'll pay to get me back. But if you hurt me, the full measure of the law will come down on you."

I didn't really know what I was saying, but I was trying to sound impressive. My parents had money and would pay to get me back, but I knew they'd have the man arrested.

The teen would go to some juvenile detention center. What would happen to the kid? As mean as it was to be the bait, maybe he was too little to know any better.

While I talked, all three of them stared at me like I was something holy, like an angel of the Lord.

"We won't hurt you," the man said. But he acted nervous, huffing and shifting his weight around, and that worried me. He didn't seem to know what he wanted to do with me.

"Why me?" I said again, but none of them would look me in the eyes. It was probably a silly question. I'd been all alone in the empty early-morning city, and I'd have followed that little boy wherever he led me. It could have happened to anyone.

"We promise we won't hurt you," the teen boy said. His voice shook when he talked to me. I wondered if he thought I was pretty, so I figured I should be extra nice to him in case it inspired him to free me when his dad wasn't looking.

"We'll untie you as soon as we can," the man said. "We just need to be sure you won't run off. Come on inside and meet my wife, the boys' mother. She's Mrs. French."

The man wouldn't untie my ankles or wrists, so he had to carry me down the weedy path to the house and over the three steps that led up to the front porch.

My mind raced around, wondering if the police were looking for me yet. But no one knew where I was. Even by the time my bosses got to work, they might figure I was running late.

The idea of them frowning about me filled my stomach with knots. If I promised I wouldn't report the crime in exchange for my release (and somehow managed to hide the whole thing from my parents), I'd still have to make up some excuse for why I wasn't at work on time. I know I should have just been thinking about my safety, but I could hardly believe what was happening to me. It didn't seem real.

The inside of their house was even more rundown than the outside. It looked like they tried their best to keep clean and orderly without having much money to spend. The curtains and couch were probably thirty years old, and everything else was even older than that. The walls and hardwood floors were all nicked. It reminded me of my Aunt Ginger's house. She's my mom's sister, though my mom tries her to best to avoid her. We used to go over there on Christmas Day, and we'd give her kids nice toys while they gave us something homemade like paper dolls or little kid drawings. My older sister was nice about it since she knew they didn't have much money to spare, but I always cried when I got my present. I can't help but get excited about presents, no matter who they're from.

"Here, sit down," the man said, motioning towards the couch. I did as he asked, seeing no better alternative. Once I was settled, he went to the stairs and called out, "She's here!"

That was the worst part of all. When he said, "she," I could tell he meant me in particular. Not just any random woman you might kidnap from the city.

"Like I said, my family will pay anything," I reminded him. Tears gathered in my eyes, and I let them.

They stared at me as I cried, but none of them said anything comforting. While wiping away my tears, I studied their appearances in case I needed to describe them to the police. All three had lank blond hair and big brown eyes with eyelashes so dark it looked like they were wearing makeup. Their hair looked home-cut, a little askew. The man and teen boy wore clean jeans and short-sleeve button-down shirts. They even looked like they could be office workers since it was casual Friday. I never went casual, of course, because I didn't see the fun in it.

I looked down and saw that the blue blazer I'd bought the previous weekend was smudged on the left lapel with grease from their trunk. My anguish over such a small thing surprised me. My life was in danger, maybe, and it's not like I thought my blazer was more important than my life. But it was something I could see, and it was most definitely ruined.

"What's wrong? Are you hurt?" the man said after I made that strange sound.

Before he could answer, the woman of the house descended the stairs. The guys who had captured me were so sleepy and plain, I knew they couldn't be the masterminds. I was sure the woman would be a cold-blooded witch.

When she came all the way down and I got a good look at her, I was surprised by how timid she was. She was wearing a plain dress that could have been a nightgown, and her frizzy brown hair was in a ponytail. I guessed she was my mother's age. Like the guys who'd taken me, she looked at me with admiration, like I was special.

Most people I knew were pleasant to me and treated me like a nice girl, but this was something else. These people seemed to already know me on the inside, like they knew my favorite movie was an old one called Fried Green Tomatoes, and my favorite restaurant was Lost Sea over in Five Points, and that I loved Gulf Shores and Christmas decorations more than anything, and that my best friend was Hadley Whittaker. Guys at parties sometimes looked at me that way, but I'd finally figured out they were lying. They made assumptions about who I was and what I liked based on how I looked, and sometimes they were right, but just as many times, they were dead wrong.

"What do you want from me?" I said. "You think it's normal to tie someone up and throw them in your trunk? You're acting like this is no big deal!"

"We know this isn't normal," Mrs. French said. She gave a tiny bow in my direction. "This is not how we want to do things. We're just following orders."

"Whose orders?"

"We'll help you get in touch with your family and your office so they won't worry," she said, ignoring my question. She hovered over me without touching me, like a moth circling a light.

"But please let me go." I began to sob. The only explanation was these people were psychotic, and you couldn't trust anything a psychotic person told you.

"We will. But first we need your help with something." She came close to me and put her hand on my cheek like she was my mother. I couldn't help but appreciate the gesture.

"What do you want me to do?" If I cooperated quickly, maybe they'd let me go that morning.

"Before we get into that, why don't you take this pill?" the man said, offering me a tiny white one from his giant palm.

"What is it?"

"Just something to calm you down.

We need you to be in the right state of mind."

I'd borrowed my friend's meds before, and I recognized the pill he offered me when I picked it up and examined it. What could it hurt? The teen boy handed me a glass of water, which I had to hold precariously since my wrists were bound.

"Okay, I took it. Could you untie me now?"

"Remember, we said we'd entertain her while waiting for that pill to kick in," Mrs. French whispered to her husband.

"Sure thing," the man said. "Let me introduce myself. I'm Mr. French, but you can call me Otto. This here is my eldest boy, John, and this is our youngest fellow, Seth."

Seth had been hiding behind his father, but he peeked out at me, and I looked mournfully at his pitiful little face. He was the cause of all my troubles. Why did I have to be such a sucker for kids?

"Where am I?" I'd been so scared on the car ride, I wasn't able to pay attention to how long it had lasted. It had seemed like a long time.

"We're way out in the country," Otto said. He gave me such a broad smile, he reminded me of a salesman. "But you probably already figured that. It's better if you don't know exactly yet. I'd tell you, but you wouldn't like it in the long run. We just need to give you a little time to get adjusted. Then you'll understand."

"But you promise you won't hurt me?" I could feel the pill kicking in a little. Or at least, I was comforted that I'd taken the pill. In spite of everything, I felt myself relax a little.

"I swear by God's throne," the man said.

That was a good sign. He was probably religious. I leaned back on the couch and looked around at the dismal little living room thinking they must have needed ransom money pretty badly.

I was sitting on a urine-colored velveteen couch, and there were two worn recliners across from me. No one else seemed to feel like sitting down. On the coffee table was a thick book with pictures of space, the only object that looked almost new. It was one of those photography books you might see at the library, something nobody really sat down and read. What did they want with a big book like that? Little toy cars were scattered around all over the floor, probably by little Seth. That mean little kid. Maybe I'd steal a couple on my way out to teach him a lesson about tricking nice folks who were on the way to work. It didn't seem like anyone in this family was going to work, unless kidnapping people was their occupation.

The dad must have noticed I was staring at his kids with a bitter look on my face, because he told them to sit down on the ugly chairs and stop staring at me. He sat down beside me on the couch, and his wife went into the kitchen to get us all some apple cider and pie. As if I felt like eating.

"If this is some kind of weird sexual thing, I'll never go along with it," I whispered, trying to protect little Seth from impropriety.

"Oh my Lord, no," the man said, blushing as if he were a little kid. "You've been living in that degenerate city too long. You've forgotten how it is out here among us simple folks."

His accent was a little strange. Country, but somehow more old-fashioned than I'd heard before. These people acted like relics from a bygone time, like people in a black-and-white movie.

"How can I trust you not to be creepy when this is the creepiest thing that ever happened to me?" I said, hoping to shame him a little. It worked.

He clasped his hands and looked down at the crotch of his pants. "I wish to God I didn't have to do it this way. I wouldn't have done it unless I'd been under the strictest orders."

"Who gave you orders to kidnap me?" I tried to think of all my enemies. One or two girls from college hated my guts, and I had a couple of disgruntled ex-boyfriends, but I couldn't imagine any of them hiring a country family to kidnap me.

He seemed to be having a conversation with himself, but finally, he shook his head. Instead of answering me, he stood up and clicked a knob on the TV, which looked about forty years old. Loud static filled the room, and I unsuccessfully tried to cover my ears with my tied-up hands.

"Sorry, sorry," he muttered, twisting the volume knob and messing with a dusty-looking VCR on top of the TV.

I was half-expecting some kind of cult initiation video, but when the tape started to play, it was just The Sound of Music. It was one of the only movies my grandmother had owned when I was a little kid, so I'd watched it quite a bit. I'd always disliked it for being so long and full of old songs, but when you're a kid, you have slim pickings.

Mr. French looked back at me with a smile so big I could have counted all his teeth if I'd wanted. "You'll love this," he said, like he was showing me something new.

At first, I tried to find a hidden message in the movie. Were these people going to take me to a convent to be a nun like

Maria was at the beginning of the movie? Or were they going to make me be their nanny like Maria became later? I shuddered to think that Mr. French was looking for a new wife, a mother for his kids. I found Maria so annoying, anyway. Wearing rumply mountain clothes and singing about kittens wasn't my idea of a good time.

To my surprise, the rest of the family loved watching the movie. They sang along with the songs, doe a deer and all. The only one who looked even a little embarrassed was John, who buried his face in his hands sometimes and laughed. He swayed in a way that looked inadvertent, as if he was on something and couldn't stay awake. I wondered if he'd taken a pill, too.

I whispered very softly to him so the others couldn't hear. "Can you free me? Please?" I had to try.

He swatted at his ear like he was trying to kill a fly, and he wouldn't turn back to look at me even though I asked nicely several times.

Giving up on John for the moment, I decided to break the spell of movie-watching to see if they'd give me any more information. "Why are we watching this? Are you trying to teach me about family values?"

They all looked at me like I'd bleached my eyebrows.

"This is a great movie!" Otto said. "Don't you remember it?"

"Of course, but I don't really like it," I said. "I know it's important because it's about Nazis. Anything with Nazis is important, because we have to remember what they did so that no one does it again." After all, did these people think I was as ignorant as they were?

"What are Nazis?" Seth said, but he asked his mother and not me, like he wasn't supposed to talk to me.

"Bad people," his mother said. "They killed millions and millions of people. They tried to destroy the whole world. They wanted to tell everyone what to do."

"But you tell me what to do," he said.

"Not very often," John said so quietly that I thought it was meant only for my ears.

"It's different for a kid. But grown-ups can't be making each other do everything," Mrs. French said.

I wondered if she realized how strange it was to talk about how wrong coercion was when I was sitting right there, being coerced into going to their house to watch a boring old movie. I ventured to clear my throat, and Mrs. French managed to blush a little. She told the boy to keep quiet and watch the movie.

Nothing we said made a difference to Otto. His eyes were glued to the fuzzy TV set like he was a little kid watching his favorite cartoon.

During the goodnight song that the kids sing at the fancy party (which would honestly be humiliating to experience in real life), John burped. Loudly. His mother scolded him, and he apologized in a voice that didn't sound sorry to me.

At some point after things got bleak in the movie world, Mrs. French stood up. "Time for some treats!" she announced like she was saying "come and get it" to a bunch of hogs. By that point, I was naturally rather put out by the whole family. You can't blame me for thinking mean thoughts about them, can you?

I thought her kids would act up while she was in the kitchen and no one was keeping an eye on them, but they kept watching the movie like they found it interesting. The idea of a big happy family sitting around and watching a movie in silence was strange to me. My family is happy as families go, but we've always fought during movies. One of us talks too much, and another is too silent. Someone spills popcorn on the floor or wipes a smear of fake butter on the couch. I always get in trouble for losing focus during the movie and singing a little song to myself. I just happen to think full-length movies are too long given these fast-paced times. They need to make shorter movies.

Mrs. French brought us all mugs of steaming apple cider and giant hunks of pecan pie. Everyone else chugged down the drink and devoured the pie, but I was too nervous to be hungry. Besides, I don't like pecans. The mug was nice and warm, though, and the cider smelled comforting. I wondered who was going to help me to the bathroom since I was tied up, but I decided to drink anyway. I was starting to feel like I was at my grandmother's house, like I was a kid again. Being a kid is like always being kidnapped and forced to do stuff against your will.

The trouble is, if a victim doesn't try hard enough to escape, I know what people say about them. Maybe I should have tried harder, but the way I saw it, it was impossible. Mr. French was huge, and I could see his gun cabinet was near the front door. Even if I hadn't been all tied up, I wasn't a very fast runner. I didn't want to get hurt or killed. My freedom in that moment wasn't worth risking my life.

Plus they must have slipped something in my mug, because I started feeling warm and safe and sleepy. So drowsy. I didn't notice the moment I fell into sleep and left the movie behind.

When I woke up, I was covered in sweat. The room was mostly dark, with the reddish late afternoon sun peeking through the closed blinds. They'd covered me with a whole pile of blankets that were scratchy and smelled like sour milk. I tossed them off into a heap on the floor and tried to catch my breath. In my sleep, I'd convinced myself that the kidnapping was a bad dream.

I had to go to the bathroom, so I called out for Mrs. French. She came running in from the kitchen with a look of fear, like I was going to curse her or something.

"I need to go to the bathroom," I said, and she seemed relieved.

"We decided that once you woke up, we'd untie you."

"Oh, good!" I was happy, and yet to be honest, it also sort of scared me. If I was free, maybe I was supposed to make a run for it. I still didn't think I had much chance of getting away and making it back to town, and I still didn't feel like a daredevil.

"We're going to let you spend some time upstairs in the bedroom. It's normally where Otto and I sleep, the best room in the house.

It has a bathroom, and I put some old documents and keepsakes up there for you to look at."

"I don't know what you're talking about. Why would I want to look through your old stuff?"

She blushed a little, and I felt guilty for being insulting, but I had no desire to rifle through some musty old papers. Instead of answering, she led me up the stairs and into a little bedroom with an attached bathroom. I had to go to the bathroom so urgently, I didn't think about much else. Mrs. French cut the ropes, and I saw I had some scrapes on my wrists and legs. After I went to the bathroom, I washed the blood away and got a few smudges of red on the white guest towels, which I would have felt guilty about under different circumstances.

I'd assumed Mrs. French was waiting outside the bathroom door for me, but when I opened the bathroom door, she was gone. The bedroom was empty. The door to the hall was shut and wouldn't open when I pulled at the knob. I looked through the keyhole and saw Mrs. French's wide brown eye. The nerve of her! She'd locked me in.

"I put a bottle of bubble bath by the tub if you feel like having a soak. Of course, you can't get out. We nailed the windows shut."

"Why on earth?" I wasn't going to jump out of a second story window anyway, but it made me feel claustrophobic to be shut in.

"Just trust us. There are some important keepsakes and old documents up there. I put them in a folder. Please go through them when you get a chance."

"But what about my parents? My boss? They'll call the police!"

I hoped that was true, but sometimes I skipped off to the beach with my friends for the weekend without telling my parents, and sometimes I called in sick to work on Fridays. Everyone I worked with liked to go to the lake on the weekends, so the office usually emptied out by lunchtime on Friday. I wished I'd established a better pattern of always being where I said I was going to be. Still, I was sure the police would be hunting me before too long.

"We used your phone to send text messages to your mother and your supervisor. They both responded in a real friendly way. No one is worried, so there's no need for you to worry.

How did they get my password? They lived in the past, it seemed to me, so I didn't think they'd even know how to use a phone. I began to feel a raging tightness inside, like a small animal was trapped in my heart and clawing to get out. How could something like this have happened to me? I backed away from the door and let myself collapse onto the dusty old bed. The mattress was hard as cement, and it creaked when I fell into it. I curled up into a ball and let myself cry, or maybe even forced myself. In a way, I was still too shocked to fully feel what had happened to me, but I knew enough to cry about it.

They had been seeking me out in particular, singling me out. Was this bad luck, or a punishment from God? I said a prayer asking for forgiveness just in case I'd sinned. Nothing this bad had ever happened to me before, and it just didn't make sense. I mean, I'd been dumped a couple of times and my best friend in middle school stole my boyfriend, and I'd gotten so drunk in college that I had my stomach pumped (just twice), and my dad got really sick when I was a little kid (but he got better). A couple of my guys I met at parties were pretty awful to me, but they were out of the picture. Maybe I didn't always feel lucky, but I knew as I cried on that rock-hard bed that I'd been lucky my whole life. Some of my friends loved true crime shows, but they gave me the creeps. I tried not to watch sad movies. Life was hard enough, at a certain level, so it didn't make sense to wallow in sorrow. Otherwise, you wouldn't be able to put one foot in front of the other.

"Maybe this is to punish me for not appreciating my good luck before," I said to myself. I sat up in bed and felt a tingle of hope.

I said a little prayer apologizing to God for that specific sin, and I started to feel better. With all my prayers, things would work out. And whether Mrs. French was lying about the texts to my mom and boss or not, I knew my friends would start texting me before too long, and those rednecks couldn't trick them into thinking they were me. The police would find a trail. If only I'd had breadcrumbs to leave like Hansel and Gretel. I hadn't even thought to leave any kind of signal. On TV, people are resourceful in the face of violence and crime, but my strength has never been in outsmarting people. My strength has always been in charming them. I've rarely found myself in situations I couldn't talk myself out of.

This was a tough case, though. These people were so certain they needed something from me, but they wouldn't tell me what. I pulled myself together so I could get up and read the documents that Mrs. French wanted me to read. Maybe I could figure out what they wanted me to do.

The room had an antique-looking desk and chair where I took my place as if I were at work. Beside a battered old file folder (couldn't they even afford new folders?), she'd left me a little wicker basket full of oranges and blueberry muffins. She'd also left me a big glass of water on the desk beside two little white anxiety pills. I was too nervous to eat, so I took the pills. No reason to be terrified if I didn't have to be.

Inside the folder, there was a homemade booklet that looked like the cheaply-printed books of bad recipes that churches sell for fundraisers. Except this little book was called Star Shapes, with a crude drawing of a shooting star on the fingerprint-smudged cover. The book was twenty-two pages, and each page had a drawing of a made-up constellation on it. I know nothing about space, so none of the stars looked familiar to me. Whoever had made this book (Mr. or Mrs. French?) might have sat outside at night and copied the stars they saw, or they might have written it indoors in broad daylight and just made up where all the stars were. I wouldn't have known the difference.

On the first page, the constellation was "the egg," labeled in all lowercase letters. It had just five stars, and it didn't look like an egg to me. But to be honest, the real constellations don't ever look like anything to me. The Big Dipper might be the only exception, once you see it.

After the egg was the squash, the tomato, the snake, the ant, the dog, the camellia, the broom, the shovel, the ivy, and the pine tree.

Then a page break, and a section two. In this section, there was the rocking chair, the frying pan, the book, the shotgun, the hat, the ring, the cup, the needle, the quilt, the pie, and the eyeglasses.

All the drawings looked like they'd been done by someone who'd at least taken Intro to Art. Each one had some sense of perspective, and the sketch of the camellia was especially loving. But there were no words to explain it all, and I didn't know what to think, so I put the book aside and hoped it wasn't too important.

Beneath the book, I found a couple of blurry-looking photographs. One was of a woman holding a baby. She and the baby were standing in a patch of happy sunlight, but they both looked grim. I didn't recognize them. Another was a black-and-white photo of a creepy-looking farmhouse.

Behind the pictures was a handwritten recipe for pecan pie. Probably the recipe for the pie that Mrs. French tried to make me eat earlier. Corn syrup. Pecans. Flour. So what?

I put it aside and read over the last piece of writing in the folder, which was a poem or a prayer written on a yellowed sheet of paper in the same handwriting as the pecan pie recipe.

I will eat the egg, the tomato, the squash, the pie.
I will feed the snake, the ant, the dog.
I will work with the broom, the shovel, the frying pan, the needle.
I will decorate with the camellia, the ivy, the pine tree.
I will rest with the rocking chair, the quilt, the book, the cup.
I will wear the hat, the ring, the eyeglasses, the shotgun.

I'd never liked to be creeped out, and something about this list of items was so creepy, I wanted to slide the book back under the door so Mrs. French could take it away from me.

Did she want me to say the prayer to myself so she could convert me to her weird religion? Whether people believe in nothing or science or some alien or God, they all want to convert you. I've never been much for arguing, but I'm also not someone who joins a bunch of causes and churches. I dated a guy like that. You could sell him almost anything. I sold him on the idea of our relationship. I had to break up with him, though, because he was always dragging me to environmental meetings, and we had to be so careful about everything, recycling every scrap of plastic. Buying anything took a million years, because we had to check the ethics and the testing and the environmental impact. I cared about helping the planet, but he was trying to do something impossible. When I told him why I was breaking up with him, he cited a bunch of statistics and told me I was selfish. Even months after we broke up, he was still sending me articles about glaciers.

I've never been easy to convert. I would have been a good actress, because I can give people this look—I don't know quite how I do it—but it makes them feel like I believe them. People always think I agree with them, that I vote however they vote for, that I worship however and whoever they worship. But inside, I can easily disagree with them. Whatever someone believes, I believe something a little different. There's no way I pray to the same God that you do.

I closed the folder and looked around the room to see if I could find any other hints about why I was there. They'd cleaned out the room very well, though. I'd have expected to find a Bible, but no luck. She must have wanted me to keep staring at those twenty-two shapes, to study them over and over. No way!

Instead, I took a bubble bath, which gave me the fleeting feeling that I was vacationing at a subpar bed and breakfast.

When I emerged and returned to my room, I found a dinner tray had been left on the desk. Someone had managed to sneak in without my hearing anything at all. The house and all its inhabitants were creepy, yet I was growing used to their weird ways the way Alice got used to Humpty-Dumpty and the Cheshire Cat.

The light through the window had already faded. I looked out over the sprawling farmland and couldn't help but admire its beauty, even in the dismal state I was in. All around were golden fields of empty stalks, with forests and rolling hills in the distance. I'd been on a few camping trips out in the boondocks, and I hadn't enjoyed myself since there were spiders and crickets and snakes (or the danger of them), but there was no denying it was beautiful out there in the daytime. The night was coming soon with its shadows and monsters.

No use thinking about that. I was hungry when I sat down at the desk, and the greasy food smelled good. If anyone needed comfort, it was me right then.

I picked up a fried chicken leg, still hot, and devoured it. It always seemed strange to me to eat meat off the bone, like I was a lion gnawing at a gazelle. But I hadn't eaten much all day, and I was starving, and there was no one to see me. Mrs. French hadn't given me too much food, maybe because they didn't have much to spare. Or maybe she didn't want me to be sick. That was more likely since she'd offered me so many little treats throughout the day.

As sides, she'd given me two halves of a deviled egg and a pile of cooked vegetables. Zucchini. Onions. Squash. Tomatoes.

Oh, not those. Not squash and tomatoes. Those were in the book, in the prayer. I was not going to eat those. They might be cursed or something. I ate the zucchini and onions but left those star shapes uneaten, even though they looked soft and buttery. I loved deviled eggs, and I'd almost bitten into one of those right away, but fortunately I'd stopped myself. The egg was the very first of the star shapes. I didn't want to go through any of their rituals, so I would have to be vigilant. I put the tray on the floor beside the door, figuring someone would grab it when my back was turned.

I thought about crying some more, but I began to feel a warm, sleepy feeling again, and I realized they had probably slipped something into my food. I almost welcomed it. I needed to escape from the situation. I crawled under the musty old covers and went to sleep.

When I woke up, the bright light of mid-morning was streaming through the window. I'd spent so much of the previous twenty-four hours asleep, but I didn't want to be awake. I didn't have any idea of how I was going to escape my imprisonment.

My dinner tray had been taken and a breakfast tray placed on my desk. It had a biscuit with jam and a glass of milk. As I was finishing up, I heard someone whisper through my keyhole.

"Are you awake?"

"I'm awake. Who is it?"'

"It's me, Seth." He sounded like he was about to tell me a secret. I had been wrong to trust him before, but once I was caught, I was caught. I had nowhere to be, so I might as well listen.

"What do you want?" I said.

"I don't know."

"Why did you help your family kidnap me? That was very mean of you."

"I just did what they told me to do. They said I had to help."

"Are they going to hurt me?"

He paused, as if considering the question. "No. You're the one who's going to do the hurting, I think."

"What do you mean?"

"I'm not supposed to say. You have to get used to being here first."

I heard Mrs. French shouting from downstairs.

"You get away from that door, Seth! Get down here right now!"

"Gotta go," he said, and he was gone.

Had he heard them say that I was going to hurt someone? I wondered if they were running a militia-style cult. I'd never been in a fight in my life, and I couldn't stand the sight of blood. I went to the gym, but I didn't lift weights. Surely they'd recognize they were dealing with someone who was of no use to them. But he'd probably misunderstood. It was clear he wasn't in the loop.

I pulled at the door to make sure it was still locked. When nothing happened, I knocked for a minute before I started kicking. I wasn't sure what came over me. I'd planned to wait patiently so that I could convince them I was compliant, but I was beginning to feel a sense of doom. I'd tried being nice, so maybe it was time to throw a tantrum.

In a minute, Mrs. French was at my keyhole, speaking to me in a sweet little voice, asking me to calm down.

"You've got me trapped!" I said. "Don't you realize what you're doing is illegal? And it's just plain wrong!"

"Did you look through the folder?"

"Yes! Are you trying to get me to convert to your religion? Is that what this is? Because I'll go to any kind of church service if you'll just let me go."

"It's not like that, silly girl. I mean, I'm so sorry, I don't mean to be disrespectful." She sounded grave as she apologized to me, like she was afraid of what I'd do to her.

"You don't consider kidnapping to be disrespectful, I guess."

"None of that looks familiar to you? Those star shapes?" she said.

I tried to remember how I felt when I first opened the Star Shapes book, whether I'd seen those shapes before.

"I don't think so. Should I know them from somewhere?"

She paused for a minute, her breath heavy at the keyhole. "I'll tell you what. If you let us tie you up again, we'll take you out to look at something. If enough time goes by and you really can't remember, we'll take you back downtown. If you promise not to tell on us."

"Anything! I promise anything! How long will it be before you let me go?"

"I have to talk it over with Otto. Maybe a week?"

"A week! I'll lose my job! Everyone will think I'm dead!"

"Oh no, we told them all you have the flu and will be in bed all week. Can't be around people or you'll spread it. Everyone understands."

"Oh God."

"It'll be okay. You can trust us."

Of course I couldn't trust them. But if I lost my hope, I'd be worse than dead. I had to try to believe things would work out for me just as they always had.

I opened the door, and Mrs. French tied my wrists.

"What's your first name?" I asked her, hoping to get on more familiar terms with her.

"Sandra," she said, giving me a timid smile like she was the new girl at school. It was hard to believe I was getting pushed around by someone like her.

Otto came in to lead me downstairs and to the car, where he tied my ankles before closing my door. He drove an old rundown Buick with a rusty hood, the kind you could unlock without much trouble from any seat in the car. He put me in the passenger seat beside him, and he duct-taped the lock so I couldn't touch it.

Sandra got in the backseat. They left the kids out of the trip, which I was thankful for. I didn't want to see Seth's chubby little face again, and John made me nervous for some reason.

"You aren't going to kill me, are you?" I said, preparing to cry. "I'm too young."

"Of course not! Who do you think we are?" he said, and I didn't dare answer.

"It's true," Sandra said. "You're too young to die. You haven't fulfilled your purpose. It's just beginning."

"Has anyone ever treated either of you this way? I mean, is that why you attacked me?" I said, wondering if I'd have any success psychoanalyzing my captors.

"We didn't attack you," Otto said, his sunburned forehead wrinkling.

"Nothing like this has happened to us before, and we have never done this before. It's a special situation," Sandra said.

Otto turned on the radio, probably to discourage me from talking, and he flipped to a soothing classical music station. I watched the fields full of hay bales roll by for a minute. He turned onto a dirt road, and I got nervous again. No matter what they said, this seemed like the kind of thing people did before they murdered you.

At the end of the dirt road was a house that was even more ramshackle than the one the French family lived in. It did look familiar, somehow. I closed my eyes and tried to remember where I'd seen the house before, and I wondered if it was the house from the old picture they'd given me.

When I opened my eyes, I saw an old man sitting on the porch. As we pulled up closer, he stood up from his chair and gave us a grave look.

"Who is he?" I said. I wondered how many other people they'd roped into their little cult. Maybe this man was some kind of priest I was being taken to meet.

We pulled up close to the house, but no one got out of the car.

"You don't recognize him?" Sandra said. She leaned forward, her voice in my ear. "Look at him. Look him in the eyes."

He was just an old man. Kind of short, a little stout. He had bushy gray eyebrows and a little billy goat beard. Nothing about him was interesting.

"Was he in the news or something?" My mom watched the local news, but I'd always found it so boring. Maybe I could have avoided the whole mess if I'd just paid attention to the local crime beat.

"Get a good look at him, and we'll go back home so you can think about it a little longer," Sandra said.

I stared at him for a minute, and the old man stared back. Without talking or waving to him, Otto drove away again.

"That was it? That was what you wanted to show me?" I was disappointed I wasn't going to get more of an outing. Otto pointed the car back in the direction of their house, which was only a few minutes away.

"He might not be famous to the world, but he's a significant person to our family."

"I'm not in your family," I said. "Oh, wait. Does one of you think I am? Like, that Otto had an affair with my mom or something?"

"Of course not!" Otto said, and they both reassured me that no one had had an affair. But they wouldn't elaborate, no matter how many times I asked.

"I just don't see what all this old stuff has to do with me," I said. "Why drag me into it?"

"Old stuff always comes back to haunt us. Each and every one of us. No one is safe from old stuff," Otto said.

"But not all the old stuff in the world."

"You never know," Sandra said. "You never know what old stuff is yours. It's like the Nazis."

"What do you mean?" I said.

She shook her head and refused to explain what she meant, which was maddening. I was dying to know. Were these people descended from Nazis? It wouldn't have surprised me a bit.

Of course, everyone's descended from someone evil. But what can you do to change something that happened before you were born? These people were stuck, which was their problem. But to understand them, it seemed I was going to have to understand their dull old past.

"How can I cooperate when you tell me so little?" I said as they untied my ankles. Otto kept his big bear hands on my shoulders as he guided me into the house, but this time I noticed a big rocking chair on the porch.

"Is this the chair from the Star Shapes book?" I said.

Otto stopped pushing me, and Sandra clapped her hands.

"You remember!" she said.

"Oh. Yeah." Maybe if I went along with them, they'd start to listen to me. "It's up in the stars, too."

"It's hard to say whether the chair existed first or the star shape existed first. Maybe the chair inspired the shape, or maybe the shape inspired the chair. But they are related. There's no doubt in my mind." Sandra regarded the chair like it was a throne.

"Can I sit in it?" I said, testing to see if they thought I was worthy to sit in the special chair (which had cobwebs wrapped around its legs and smelled like mildew).

"Oh yes. That would be wonderful," Sandra said. "Just be careful. It's easy to forget how fragile it is."

I could tell. The seat was unraveling, so I barely let my weight rest on it.

"You remember now?" Otto said. "This chair is special."

"I guess all the star shapes are special," I said. "And you gave me the tomatoes and squash and egg to eat already."

"But you wouldn't eat them."

"It's like you want to introduce me to all the shapes. You want me to know them all, to have them all?"

"Why not?" Sandra said. She gave me the kind of smile you see from women in commercials for dishwashing detergent. "It can't hurt to try!"

"Fine," I said, figuring it wouldn't cost me anything.

2.

Sandra made lunch while Otto took me around back to meet their dog. He said that since I was being good, I wouldn't have to be tied up. I think he figured out that I didn't have any escape plans other than begging. And I hoped they'd keep up their end of the bargain. Hoping was all I could do.

"The dog doesn't come inside?" I said.

"No, he likes the outdoors."

I doubted that any creature would choose the outside over the inside in the long run, but I didn't argue with him. Behind their house was a huge area with patchy grass, fenced in with warped, rusty-looking wires. A huge German Shepherd came bounding over and put his paws up on the fence trying to get to us.

"This is the dog in the Star Shapes book? I thought that one looked smaller."

Otto laughed. "You're onto something there. But keep thinking on it."

He took me to the battered gate and let me inside. The dog ran up and sniffed us all over. I tried to pet him, but he was too excited to sit still.

"His name is Popsicle." Otto grabbed Popsicle and wrestled with him, which delighted the dog.

"What am I supposed to do with him?" I said.

"First, you got to look at him and try to understand him. Try to see through what he is into something bigger."

"Oh, right." I stared at the dog with an intensity I hoped Otto appreciated.

After romping for a bit, Otto got up again. He pulled a little dog treat from his back pocket and handed it to me. I offered it to Popsicle, who went into an ecstasy and licked it out of my hand.

Otto stood beside me as I was observing Popsicle and asked me, "You believe in God, don't you?"

Here it was. The conversion speech.

"Yes."

"You go to one of those fancy Episcopal churches downtown."

"That's true." He must have been following me for some time. Or maybe he'd googled me and seen I was in the church's group for young professionals.

"You know how in the Bible, it says God made each living creature after its kind?"

"Oh, yes." It sounded like something you'd find in the Bible.

"Well, that's true. Dogs mate, and there are more dogs. People mate, and they make more people. But see, the truth is, God also remakes things after their own kind."

I tried to look impressed by this fact, but I didn't know what he was talking about.

"Just look at Popsicle. Some people have special insight. They can look at a living thing and see the past versions of it. Popsicle couldn't have been a bug or a man or a stone in a past life. He was another dog. See?"

I tried to see the past version of Popsicle within the big German Shepherd who was sniffing me all over.

"Popsicle has been with us many times. When Star Shapes was written, he was a past version of himself. Back then, he was a girl beagle. Don't you just love beagles? They're the sweetest things. Spunky, too."

"Adorable!" I was a cat person, though I'd never had time for a pet.

"Yeah. You...I think something's sparking for you. You got a little touch of a memory?" He looked at me like we were old friends, and I tried to return the look.

"Maybe I do. Maybe I do have a memory of something."

He grinned and patted my shoulder. "Well, that's a great start. I was right that we should start with Popsicle. I think you've got time to see the plants before lunch."

We were moving at a steady clip. I'd already sat in the rocking chair and fed the dog. If we could get all three plants out of the way, then I'd only have seventeen things left to check off the weird list, and maybe then they'd let me go.

He took me around to the side of the house to a lovely little enclosed garden with a picked-clean vegetable patch and sculpted bushes and flowers. A freshly-painted white fence surrounded it. The garden area was the only part of the property they seemed to freshen up on a regular basis.

A bit of English ivy wound around a trellis that was placed on the side of the house. The vine's leaves were licking the bricks.

"I love this place," I said.

Otto looked at me with delight, and I began to worry. I was naturally doing what he wanted me to do. On the other hand, who wouldn't have loved the garden? It seemed to have a touch of magic.

"Am I supposed to beautify with the plants?" I said, recalling the language of the poem.

"That's right. Beautifying is all about personal expression," he said. He handed me some small plant clippers, and I snipped off a few long strings of ivy while leaving most of the growth intact.

I looked around and saw a bush with pink flowers as carefully fluffed as a little girl's pageant dress. The center of the flower was thick with spindly yellow stamens.

I looked back at Otto to make sure it was okay, and he nodded at me like he was my dad watching me ride a bike for the first time. I clipped two of the flowers and stuck them in the center of my pile of ivy.

"These camellias are called Alabama Beauties," he said.

"Did you know it's the state flower?"

"No. Good choice."

"It sure was. You're forgetting one thing, though.

The pine tree. Come this way."

As I followed him, I couldn't help admiring the plant bits in my arms. Such vibrant greens and pinks. I'd always loved receiving flowers, but so few of my exes had gotten my hints.

He led me out of the fence, away from the garden, and my bit of joy disappeared. A number of pine trees lined the gravel driveway leading up to the house, but the bottom boughs were so tall, I didn't see how I could cut off their needles.

"How am I supposed to get up there?" If that was the catch, that I had to scurry up a tree, then I wasn't going to do it. The star shapes project would be over.

"It's not like that. Take a look at these." He pointed at the pine cones littering the ground. I had some cinnamon-scented pine cones in a bowl at my apartment. It stung me a little to remember my nice cozy apartment. Would I ever return to it?

I gathered three cones from the ground, selecting the biggest and most unblemished ones. Three more items checked off my list. I was making record time.

He led me back inside the house, and he told me to beautify wherever I liked while he helped his wife with the final touches for lunch. She'd already set the table, so I wound ivy around the place settings and arranged the pine cones and camellia blooms in the empty fruit bowl in the center of the table.

The two boys came downstairs and gave me a nervous look. It must have been very odd for them to help their father catch a young woman and tie her up, and then see her decorating the dining room table.

"It's almost lunch time," I told them, trying to pretend like everything was normal. Seth wasn't wearing his pitiful outfit anymore, but jeans and a worn-looking polo shirt.

They sat down across from me and looked at the ivy and flowers and pine cones, but they wouldn't look at me. Maybe they were ashamed of how they'd treated me but didn't know how to apologize.

Soon, Otto brought in a platter of ham, and Sandra carried rolls and deviled eggs and a dish of buttery squash and tomatoes. We all tried to act ordinary about it. I spooned all the foods onto my plate.

"I'll pray," Otto said once we had all served ourselves. "Dear Lord, please bless this time. It is a special time, Lord, the end of many years of waiting. Give us wisdom. Help us see who we really are."

He stopped, and we all said "Amen."

Three more items off the list, just like that. The deviled eggs were creamy with a hint of pickle, just like I like them. The tomatoes and squash were ripe and sweet.

"Thank you for a delicious lunch," I said when I was finished, and not even to get in their good graces. When I ate with my parents and sister, we usually went out. There was something homey and special about what we'd done, decorating the table with stuff from the yard and eating plain old food. Everyone quietly chewing, no one clamoring to speak. No one speaking at all.

"That's very kind." Sandra ducked her head and smiled.

"Are we having pie for dessert?" I said, hoping to cross another item off my list.

"Not yet," Sandra said. "I thought we could make it together after you see our other pets. Seth, what if you take her to meet your ants first?"

"Yes, I guess the time has come," Seth said. His voice took on a gravity that made him sound like a hellfire preacher. He hid a roll in a paper napkin and jammed it in his pocket before leading me up to his room, where I had to be careful not to step on any tiny cars. They were everywhere, like the floor was a miniature traffic jam.

"Where'd you get all these cars?" I didn't see how his family could afford endless toys for him if they couldn't afford new curtains or a coat of paint.

"They're rewards."

"Who's rewarding you? For what?" I wanted to make him feel like he didn't deserve it.

"It's from a bequest. I get them for doing good," he said.

"A bequest? From someone who died? Who?"

"I'm not supposed to say."

He led me to his ant farm, which sat on a dusty old chest of drawers that looked a hundred years old (but not in a good way).

"These are your friends?" I was implying they were his only friends. I don't know why I was being so mean to him. Even if he was the bait, it wasn't his fault. He was too young to have made that kind of choice. I would have done anything for a toy when I was his age.

"Yeah." He didn't seem to care what I thought about him, anyway. "But there are too many to name, so they don't have names."

He unwrapped the napkin and handed me a bit of roll.

"Feed them.' He opened the top of the glass case, and the ants seemed to look up at me like I was there to save them. They waved their little antennae.

I would have to feed them like the poem said. And then I'd have to feed a snake. Of course, I hated snakes, and I didn't know if I could feed one a slimy rat or whatever they ate. But one thing at a time. One shape at a time.

I took the little piece of roll and crushed it into crumbs that I sprinkled over the top layer of sand. The ants were invigorated, and they got to work right away carrying this new source of food around.

Seth gave them some crumbs, too. "They're pretty cool," he said, staring at them in rapture. Some of them had ingested pieces of the sugary roll, and their limbs were twitching with excitement.

"Why is there an ant in the Star Shapes book? Why are ants important?"

Seth looked up at me like I was trying to steal one of his cars.

"You're supposed to know that already. You're supposed to know a lot of things you don't know. I wonder if you're the right person. Mom and Dad was sure of it, but they might have mixed something up."

"The right person for what? What are they going to do to me?"

"Do to you?" Seth said. "What do you mean?"

"Okay!" we heard Otto's booming voice behind us.

"Looks like you're finished with that one! Now it's off to feed the snake. Come along!"

Having no choice, I followed him down the hall. I glanced back to wave at Seth, but he wasn't even looking at me. He was staring at his ants, watching them carry their crumbs.

As I followed Otto, I felt like I could hardly contain myself. I knew I shouldn't question him, but I couldn't help it.

"Otto, why did y'all think I was the right one? Right for what?"

He turned around to look me in the eyes. "If you're right, then you'll know it. If you're not, then that's that. Now follow me."

I jumped back, feeling scolded. I hoped I wasn't right the way they thought I was, of course, and yet I wondered what it meant to be right under these circumstances. If they thought I wasn't right for them, would it feel like being dumped by a loser?

Past the bedroom where they were keeping me was John's room. He was standing there holding a snake with a pretty rust-colored design on its back. The snake lifted its head and licked the air when we entered the room.

"I don't like snakes," I said.

"John will take care of you," Otto said. "Excuse me a minute."

He slammed the door shut, and a few minutes later, we heard him yelling in the other room. I almost felt guilty. I'd made Seth talk to me about the situation, and now he was getting in trouble.

"Is he going to hit him?" I said.

"Oh, no, that's never happened. I mean, they're on edge right now, but I don't think they'd go that far."

"Have you ever kidnapped a girl before?"

John's cheeks reddened, and he looked away from me. "No, definitely not. My parents are weird, but they aren't that weird. This is something different."

"They made y'all promise not to tell me?"

"Yeah. Promises around here are pretty serious."

The snake kept pointing its beady eyes in my direction.

"Can you put it away? Do I have to touch it?"

"His name is Anthem."

John took him over to a tank in the corner of his room and slid him onto a little branch that was in there. The snake slithered down and hid behind some fake-looking rocks.

"What happens if you break a promise here?" I said. John was being surprisingly candid, and I wanted to get as much as I could out of him before his father came back.

"You'll get a curse laid on you. To be honest, I have my doubts about all that. But it is embarrassing, because they make a mark on your hand, and it's hard to explain to people.

"Has anyone in your family been marked?"

"My mom. Hers is faded now. Just a scar."

I felt sick. So there were physical punishments. I resolved to be more careful in my investigations, to focus on getting out as safely as possible.

"Your dad...so he's sometimes violent. Has he ever hurt you?"

He looked back at me, still lingering by the snake tank.

"No, dad wasn't the one who gave her the mark. She did it to herself. That's how serious they take promises. She wanted to punish herself because she promised to get someone back that she couldn't get back. That was a long time ago. I was a little kid."

"Oh. Well, maybe they take promises too seriously."

"Maybe. I have my doubts about the whole thing sometimes. It looks to me like they made a mistake here, but they won't give up. They're insisting on showing you all these weird things. Like it's going to make a big difference."

"But they won't hurt me."

"Oh, no," he said, but the way he glanced back at me made me wonder. His eyes were wide. I guessed that he wasn't quite sure what they would do. The yelling in the other room died down at last, and we heard Seth wailing.

"Better hurry up and feed him." John said, motioning me over and pointing to a dead mouse that was lying beside the tank.

"Yuck!"

"I defrosted him already. All you have to do is sort of dangle him down there. To make Anthem feel like he caught it himself."

As quickly as I could, I did what he said. I dangled the mouse by the very tip of his tail, and Anthem studied it a minute before lunging. I released the mouse and looked away.

Otto opened the door again. His face was fiery red, and he looked angrily at me.

"Fed the snake?"

"Yep," I said. "I'd like to wash my hands."

He took me to the bathroom and watched me scrub and scrub my hands without saying a word. Then he led me downstairs to Sandra, who was measuring out flour and sugar into a big bowl.

"What happened up there?" she said in kind of a mumble to her husband, like I was a kid and she was talking over my head.

"Seth being unwise. Forgetful." Otto pulled a little red toy car from his pocket. "Had to teach him a lesson"

"Poor thing," Sandra said.

"He has to learn to mind. Every kid has to learn," Otto said. "Anyway, I need to go out and chop some wood. I'll be back soon."

He left us alone in the kitchen, and Sandra gave me a secret smile. "We don't need any more wood," she said. "That's what he does when he's upset. Seth must have gotten on his nerves real bad. What'd Seth tell you?"

"Oh, I was asking him. It was my fault. I was trying to find out why I was here."

"That's only natural. No one faults you for that. But the boys know better. They know that we're trying to do the right thing here, and that we're following a plan. Without that plan, everything will be chaos. We need plans to keep things in order. Sometimes we want to mistrust the one who gives us the plans. That's how man felt in the Garden of Eden. That's why we ate the forbidden fruit."

"Oh yeah," I said.

"I'm sure everything is going to come together real soon. But our next step is a fun one. Pie-making! Are you a baker?"

"No, I hate cooking. I can only cook buttered noodles. And I don't even like to do that. I either make the noodles too hard or too soft."

"Like Goldilocks."

"I guess." Too hot or too cold. Rarely was anything just right.

"I think it'll come naturally to you once you get started. Here, what if you use this pastry cutter to mix the butter into the flour for the crust?"

I did as she said, though it was a messy and unpleasant business. I cut myself trying to get the buttered flour chunks off the blades.

"Oh, poor thing!"

She washed my hands off and gave me a bandage. My mother used to treat me that way when I was a little kid.

"Did you always want a daughter?" I guessed.

Mouth trembling, the woman stepped back. "You know about my daughter?"

"Uh, no. You were just treating me like a daughter. I didn't mean to upset you. Did you have a daughter?"

She turned away and braced herself against the cabinet. "I did. She passed on, and we weren't able to find her again."

"Oh! I'm so sorry. I didn't mean to bring up something sad. I really didn't mean to."

I concentrated more on trying to make the butter stick to the flour. I felt so awkward, there was no way I was going to ask her any more questions about it. Even though the way she said they couldn't find her daughter sounded like the beginning of a long story.

"I still feel guilty. I just wish I'd known what was going to happen. I wish I'd been told." She turned around and looked at me as though I were the one who should have told her.

"I'm so sorry about that. I'm so sorry." For a minute, I felt like I was suffocating in her pain and disappointment, even though I was avoiding eye contact with her.

Sandra breathed deeply a few times and seemed to pull herself together. Then she came over to me and helped me finish my pie crust, adding water and smushing it all together and then rolling it out properly.

"Nevermind, then. You don't know what I'm talking about. Let's focus on the happy things. Like making this pie."

"Yeah, it's like being a kid again, messing around with clay."

She forced a laugh, and I felt more at ease. The awkward part was over. I hate bringing up uncomfortable topics. And yet, I was extremely curious about what had happened to her daughter.

It sounded like she'd run away or been lost somehow. Maybe her body had never been found.

If her daughter had been lost as a little girl, maybe she thought I was who her daughter had grown up to be. The thought filled me with dread as Sandra showed me how to shape the pie crust, and I got so anxious, I couldn't concentrate. She had to redo it for me, pressing and pinching, pressing and pinching. I didn't want to learn to make a pie crust.

I'd seen my birth certificate. I was my mother's daughter.

Unless there was some mistake. Maybe the certificate had been forged or altered. What if my parents stole me from this family and passed me off as their own? I hadn't seen many pictures from when I was very young, but my mother had said I wouldn't sit still long enough for a nice picture. What if that was a lie?

Oh, but no. I had my mother's nose. Didn't I? Or did I have Sandra's nose?

"Now, this recipe has been in my husband's family for generations. I admit, it's not so different from most pecan pie recipes, but there are some secret additions that aren't included when the recipe is written down."

I poured the little bowls of sugar and corn syrup and eggs and pecans into a larger bowl and mixed. She'd made everything so easy for me, so I didn't have to measure anything myself. Like I was on a cooking show.

She pulled a grubby old bottle of whiskey from an upper cabinet and poured in a splash.

"That's one of the secrets!" she said, smiling, and I couldn't bring myself to tell her I'd seen bourbon pecan pie at half the restaurants in town.

After I mixed it up, she grated some orange zest into the bowl of pie mix. That didn't seem that special to me either.

The final "special ingredient" was a weird prayer that Sandra said over the pie before putting it in the oven.

"Help us remember. Help us to eat and eat again. Help us to gain something new each time."

"Amen," I said, giving her a smile, hoping I seemed sincere in my participation.

She gave me a sad look, though.

"Ready to clean up?" She pointed at the flour that had fallen on the floor.

I felt kind of insulted that she was asking me to do chores. Strangely enough, I thought of myself as a guest at their house, especially since they kept treating me like I was someone special. When she handed me a very old-looking broom with mostly-bare bristles and a greasy-looking handle, I remembered. The broom in Star Shapes was ragged-looking, too.

"Oh yeah. I'm supposed to work with this." I grabbed it and swept up the flour, though not very thoroughly. The broom's

shoddy bristles left big streaks of flour behind. I swept what I could into a pile and asked for a dustpan.

"No need to worry! I'll get that. You did your part. Now it's time for you to rest."

She led me back to the shabby living room couch where I'd watched The Sound of Music on their janky old TV. It felt depressing to be back there again, like I was going in circles and not making any progress.

I sat down, and she grabbed an old quilt from a hall closet and spread it over my lap.

"I'm not sleepy," I said. They hadn't drugged my lunch, it seemed.

"You don't need to sleep. You need to rest. I'm going to get you a book and a nice cup of tea."

More items! I couldn't remember all the ones I had left. After my rest, I'd have to go up and cross them off the list and see what was left. It seemed like Sandra had it all planned out for me, though. Maybe I'd be done by the end of the day and could go home that night. Or maybe by the next day, after breakfast.

First, she handed me a book.

"This is the book? From Star Shapes?"

"Yes, this is the one! You're supposed to be relaxing, though, so don't feel you have to make a deep study of it. Not right now."

The book was a worn hardcover called The Night Sky. Inside, it had a drawing of a kid with wide eyes looking up at the stars. The copyright was 1963.

The opening was hopeful. "Do you ever look up at the stars and wonder what they are? If so, you will love the science of astronomy. It is the study of the stars. Astrology, or trying to predict the future by finding patterns in the stars, is different. Astrologists try to predict the future based on old myths. Astronomers are scientists. Which would you rather be?"

"Neither," I said to myself. How was I supposed to relax with a kids' book about such a boring topic? Not that I was in the mood for relaxing. I was in the mood to cross more star shapes of the list and get away from this sad place. While I was pondering the opening lines of the book, Sandra brought me a cup of black tea in a fragile teacup patterned with pink flowers. She hadn't asked how I wanted the tea. It was too bitter for me to drink without sugar, but to humor her, I took a sip.

"Marvelous!" she said. "Oh, I almost forgot. Wait right there."

She ran up the stairs. I winced as I took another bitter sip. When she returned, she handed me an old pair of glasses with amber frames. I put them on, but they kept slipping down my nose. When I tried to read with them, everything was a blur.

"I can't see with these things on," I said.

She looked disappointed, so I apologized.

"No, it's okay. Try a little longer, then you can take them off. See if you get used to them. And...don't you like your tea?"

"Yeah. I mean, I usually drink lattes.

"I'm sorry, dear." She gave me a comforting smile.

"We don't have those here. Just see if you can get used to everything. I'll be back soon. I'm going to start on dinner. Of course, you'll help me fry something up before the end."

"How many items do I have left?"

Her smile froze.

"Should I not be keeping track?" I said.

"I'm keeping up with it for now. You just focus on relaxing."

She left me to my book and tea and glasses.

I kept the glasses on but looked over my nose so I could read without looking through the lenses. I read about how hot the stars are and how far away they are, which I already knew in a vague kind of way.

I heard a creak at the top of the stairs. Little Seth padded down in his socks, stepping as quietly as possible. When he got to the bottom of the stairs, he got on his hands and knees and crawled like a cat. He crouched under the coffee table as if that would fool his parents.

"Dad took away my car because of what you said," he whispered, his face streaked with tears.

"He was mad at you, not me." I didn't have patience for this kid anymore. He was nothing but a nuisance.

"It's your fault!"

He wasn't like the rest of the family. Their desires were so strange and mysterious to me, but Seth's motivations were obvious.

"If you help me get out of here, I'll get you all the little cars you want. Any other toy you want, too."

"How many cars?"

"Like...a hundred?"

"That's not that many."

"A thousand!"

He considered that. My parents, of course, would have been happy to spend a million dollars on tiny toy cars if it would save my life. But I doubted Seth had that much power in the house, however much he was allowed to leave his toys scattered around.

"You should leave. Go back home. You aren't the right person."

"I'm sure I'm not. Right for what, though?"

"I don't want him to take away more of my cars."

"He won't if he doesn't know what you're saying to me."

Seth poked his head out from under the table and gave me a cold look.

"Dad said we were going to get to meet our grandma. But you're nothing like a grandma. I've never had one, but I've seen them in movies. I don't like you."

"Grandma? How could I be your grandma?"

"They think when she died, her spirit went into your body. When you was a baby."

I was being held captive based on a case of mistaken identity! A hoped-for reincarnation. These people seemed like country Christian types, though, and I didn't see where they'd picked up a belief in reincarnation.

We heard footsteps on the porch, and Seth shot out of the room and into the kitchen where his mother shouted at him for running in the house. I heard the backdoor slam shut in the kitchen just as the front door was opening. In walked Otto.

His worried look passed from his face when he saw me wearing the glasses and looking at the old textbook with the teacup by my side.

"Brings back memories," he said.

He gave me a wistful look that made me squirm, so I took off the glasses.

"I can't see in these things," I said.

"Oh, right." Some of the sparkle left his eye.

Sandra joined us in the living room holding a sewing kit and a man's shirt. She handed them both to me.

"I was just wondering if you could sew this button on Otto's shirt for me?" she said.

"The needle," I remembered from the book. "Oh, but I can't sew. Sorry."

She was openly exasperated with me for the first time.

"It's just a button!" she said. "Please don't pretend like you know less than you do just to get at us."

"I'm not!" I really wasn't. I'd never learned to sew a thing. "We always take our clothes to a tailor. And our dry cleaner mends things sometimes, too. Although this wasn't a high-quality shirt to begin with, and since it looks old and worn already, it might be time to get rid of it." I paused my lecture since they didn't seem interested in my fashion tips.

"A woman who can't even sew a button?" Sandra said, looking at me with despair. "How could that be?"

"It's the modern world. No matter where you came from, you get lost in the modern world," Otto said. He hung his head.

"I'll show you how to do it," Sandra said. "Whatever happens, it's not a bad skill to have."

"I'm going to go upstairs and talk to Seth," Otto said.

"He's outside," Sandra said.

Otto headed out the front door again.

"I shouldn't have been so hard on the little guy. Maybe he was right," he said before he closed the door behind him.

As Sandra tried to teach me the tedious skill of sewing on a button, I had a hard time focusing. Practically speaking, I knew I should continue to show them I wasn't their grandma. I didn't like the things that she liked, and I didn't know how to do the things she'd done. On the other hand, a deep and ridiculous part of me always wanted to get an A. I never wanted to disappoint. If she was going to show me how to sew a button, I wanted to prove

I could do it. My mother could do it, after all, and so could my grandmother.

Of course, my dad couldn't. Still, after watching her several times, I managed to sew the button in place. It looked sloppy, but Sandra seemed comforted that she had successfully taught me a trick.

"I'm not who you think I am," I told her. "I'm really sorry you lost your mother. And your daughter. But I'm just me."

She looked at me like I was a painting hanging in a museum. Studying me.

"You might not remember your past life."

"I don't believe in past lives."

"What you believe wouldn't make any difference to the truth of the matter," she said.

"You said you'd send me back once you decided I wasn't the right person."

"I'm not sure yet. There's an important test left."

"What is it?"

"You already know too much. The more you know, the more it messes things up. We're trying to see you as you are, but it's like you're always acting. It's so strange, just the opposite of how she was. She couldn't pretend to think anything different from what she really thought for even a second. Now, she wasn't my mother, though. She was Otto's."

"I see. You want me to act natural?"

"Exactly."

Sandra put out her hand, and I took it to be polite, even though I hardly wanted to be holding her hand. She wasn't my favorite person in the world.

"Part of being polite means acting unnatural," I told her, like I was explaining to a little kid. "If everyone did what they felt at any moment, then people would hurt each other all the time, and nothing would ever get accomplished."

I was surprised at myself, but I found myself wanting to convert her to my way of thinking. Their family was annoying, but they weren't so bad. They could be like normal people if they tried.

"Some people are special. People like Jesus. When they're being who they are, then everything gets brighter. People get smarter. Things start to happen the right way," Sandra said.

"The grandma was like that?"

"Yes. She didn't live to be a grandmother, though. She died before my oldest child was born."

"She died right before I saw born. Twenty-two years ago."

"Exactly. My mother-in-law's name was Grace," Sandra said, her voice quavering a little like we were having a monumental moment. I didn't care what her name was.

"That's what y'all want to call me? But it's not my name."

"I'm not attached to her name, but we were all attached to the idea of her. The kids want a grandma. Otto wants his mother back. Grace was my spiritual advisor. Without her, I'm afraid I've gotten lost."

"I'm not any of those things."

"We have to be sure. Whether you are her or aren't her, I know this is a bad shock to you. I can't help thinking we didn't go about it the best way. But that was the plan, see. She figured it all out and told us the plan before she died. Wasn't my idea. I'm not nearly as good at discerning the stars as she was. They don't speak to me like they spoke to her. Or if they do, it's so quiet. It takes me so long to understand." She patted the frizzy hair coming out of her ponytail, but she didn't make it look any better. I hadn't met many people who seemed to care less about the way they looked than Sandra, yet she was self-conscious about not being able to read the stars.

"That book of the star shapes you showed me doesn't look right. I think it's all made up," I said.

"You didn't know Grace. She was a prophet. She predicted all kinds of things by looking at the stars. She said she was both an astronomer and an astrologer."

"I bet she didn't even know real science or astrology. She was just making things up."

"She always said people in different countries saw different shapes in the stars. Why shouldn't she see new American shapes? New Alabama shapes? Everything didn't have to be so old, she said. She said the stars could be what you loved. She saw the things she loved up there."

I was tired of hearing about what Grace had said.

"Well, let's hurry up and do the final test."

"Right after dinner. Come on, let's fry some pork chops together," she said.

The frying pan. She filled it with oil and gave me some pre-floured chops to stick in. The pan was sizzling dangerously, so I tossed one in from a distance, and some oil popped at me. I cried out, though it only hurt for a second, and Sandra took me to the sink to douse my hand in cold water.

"Watch me," she said. She picked up another chop and gently laid it in the pan. It sizzled louder, but it didn't spit. I tried to do one like she did, and it worked all right, though I still felt the tiniest sting on my little finger.

"It's easier than I thought," I said.

"If you stay with me, I can teach you all kinds of things." She gave me a big doll smile, all eager. I pulled away from her.

"I'm not very interested in cooking. I can always get takeout."

Her smile vanished, and she looked at me like I was a stranger, which was comforting to me. She changed the subject and talked about how good homemade applesauce was with pork chops, and she stirred a pot that must have been on all day. She gave me a little spoonful of the sauce to try. I'd never liked applesauce, but I had to admit her version was way better than the watery stuff I'd had from the store.

"Tastes great," I said.

"Grace taught me all her best recipes."

But I wasn't Grace, no matter what she thought. Not to brag, but I thought of myself as a smart, pretty, positive, and classy person. This Grace seemed like she was weird and boring. I'd been dragged back in time against my will. Sure, it would have been harder to be a woman back in the old days, and I felt bad for women who lived back then, but I didn't want to become one as a show of sympathy. I wanted to take advantage of the best that life had to offer me.

Soon, Sandra sent me to the table to wait for dinner. My decorations were still in place, but the flowers were already wilting. I felt like I was awaiting a prison sentence as she lit some candles and dimmed the overhead lights.

Soon, Otto and Seth came in through the front door, holding hands. Seth had gotten his car back. He clutched it in his little paw.

"Put it away for dinner, Seth," Otto said. But Seth ignored him and put the car on the table, making it zoom back and forth over the ivy vine near his plate.

Sandra brought in the food platter by platter, and she called up the stairs for John to come down.

Everyone else was sitting down and waiting to pray by the time John stumbled downstairs. If I hadn't known better, I would have thought he was drunk.

"Sorry. Took a nap, had a hard time waking up," he said, blinking into the candlelight.

"Good to get some sleep. We have a long night ahead of us," Otto said, which made me feel sick to my stomach. Then he looked at me. "Would you mind praying tonight?"

"Me?" I thought it wasn't very polite to put your guest on the spot.

"Yeah. Just speak from the heart." He gave me the warm expression of a benevolent patriarch.

I closed my eyes and said, "Dear God, help me. Help all of us see right from wrong, truth from...untruth. Help me get out of here! God, help." I opened my eyes. "Amen," I said, though no one joined me.

Asking God for help made me emotional. I needed help more than ever before, and asking for it me feel weak and bitter, knowing I wasn't going to hear God's voice come rumbling from the sky. I felt so alone. No one would even look at me after my sad prayer.

Sandra got up and spooned food onto everyone's plate. I told her I didn't feel like eating, but she gave me way too much food anyway.

Everyone else wolfed it down, but I scraped at it with my fork. I would have devoured it under different circumstances. Maybe I could find a boyfriend who cooked.

"There's a picture upstairs of a woman holding a baby. Is that Grace?" I said. I couldn't believe they thought I was the reincarnation of such a plain woman.

"Yep. And she's holding me." Otto gave a tiny proud smile. "I was her only baby. She wanted more, but she got hurt real bad and couldn't take care of any more babies."

"How did she get hurt?" I said.

"She would never exactly say. She always spoke sideways, kind of in riddles. Maybe you think that's what we're like, but she really took the cake. I had my suspicions, though. My father is a rat bastard, to tell you the truth."

I was shocked at his language since he seemed so mild. He must have shocked himself, too, because he looked down at his plate and focused on eating instead of talking to me.

I forked some tiny bites into my mouth, but it felt like eating dust since I was so worried about my next trial. Once they were halfway through eating, Otto acknowledged me again. "I know this has been hard for you. But the worst of the ordeal is almost over. Now you know who we believe you are, and so the cards are on the table. I have total faith in my mother's faith. Her ideas always steered me right. She even led me to Sandra here. She saw something special in her." He beamed at his wife, who appeared to be touched that he'd remembered something about their shared past.

"But I'm not your mother," I said.

He nodded curtly. "The remembering is hard. Whether you are or you aren't, I believe there must be something important about you. I'm not a prophet. That was my mother. That's Sandra now. I'm just a farmer, plain and simple. A nobody."

"Come on now, Otto!" Sandra said. "Don't talk about yourself that way."

"It's the truth. I don't mind. I'm someone who helps carry out plans, not one who makes them. Well, my mother made a plan, and I'm bound to carry it out. If it doesn't work out, then maybe something unseeable happened. Maybe she was right about you being her reincarnation, but she was wrong to think you could remember your past. I don't know. But I have absolute faith in her prophecies."

I was sick of listening to him reassure himself. I wanted to get the whole thing over with.

"What are you going to make me do? Sandra said y'all had one more test. What we've done so far hasn't been bad. But I have a bad feeling about this next part."

All of them acted nervous, which made me feel worse.

"The next part is hard, but if you remembered the Grace inside of you, this part would be a lot harder. With you as you are, you might not suffer as much."

As much? I didn't deserve to suffer at all. For the first time, I seriously wondered if I could outrun them and escape. They were starting to trust me. I wasn't fast, but it was getting dark outside, and maybe I could run out and hide behind a bush when they tried to find me. I remembered Popsicle, though. He'd find me in no time.

"Just tell me what I have to do."

Otto and Sandra exchanged looks.

"Go ahead and tell her," Sandra said, and I was grateful she was there. She must have thought of me as like her daughter, for all she said I was her mother-in-law.

"Well, I'm afraid of planting memories. This next part… you're going to go to another place. You know that house we took you to earlier?"

"The creepy house with the old man?"

"You didn't used to call it creepy," Otto said. He stared at me like he was trying to see the old woman inside of me. "That old man used to be your husband, I'm sad to say. It's absolutely necessary that you talk with him. He's still a rat bastard, but don't worry. He can't hurt you now."

The old man seemed harmless enough, but the house looked to be full of ghosts. Or like it might fall apart when I stepped on the porch.

"How long do I have to stay there?"

"Oh, however long it takes," Otto said. "You'll understand more when you go inside."

I put my face in my hands. What choice did I have?

"Let's get this over with."

Sandra reached over and patted my arm. "You need to eat more. For your strength."

"There's food at his house. I was the one that took it there. She's right, we need to get this over with," Otto said.

They all scattered to prepare for my trip to the house that was only five minutes away.

Sandra brought me a wide-brimmed black hat with a black velvet flower on it. I hated it, but she said I had to wear it. She also gave me a cloudy diamond engagement ring that was too big for my ring finger, so I had to wear it on my thumb.

"That'll have to do," she muttered to herself. "Grace had knobby knuckles. She said was from cracking them too much, but I don't know."

"So that's it? That's all 22 shapes?" I said. I tried to remember them all, but I hadn't committed the list to memory.

"Almost," Otto said. He went over to his gun cabinet and got out a few rifles to hand out to the family, and to my surprise, he gave me one. "Put this over your shoulder."

It had a strap on it so I could wear it like a guitar. I'd never shot a gun before, and I didn't like being so close to one. But it was in the star shapes book, part of a crazy plan that was older than I was.

Before I left, Sandra gave me a slice of pecan pie. I ate a bite, wondering if my day in their world would make me like pecans. It didn't. I stopped at the one bite. But they were satisfied with that, as if one bite of the past was enough to remember.

3.

Otto showed me how to take the gun safety off and put it on again. With the safety on, I clutched the gun like a teddy bear on the dark ride from the old farmhouse to the older farmhouse.

What if the old man was dangerous? The thought seemed more likely to me as we approached the house. Why else would Otto have given me a gun to fend him off? My hands trembled when I thought of pulling the trigger. If he decided to attack me, I really wasn't sure I had it in me to shoot him. Or that I could figure out how to point accurately and shoot him in the right place.

When I got out of the car, I expected them to go back home and leave me alone, but instead, they all took their guns and split up to cover the exits. Otto took the front door, John the back. Sandra took little Seth (the only one not holding a gun) to wait in the trees. At first, I felt touched that they were staying to protect me from the old man, but it also occurred to me they might be there to keep me from running away.

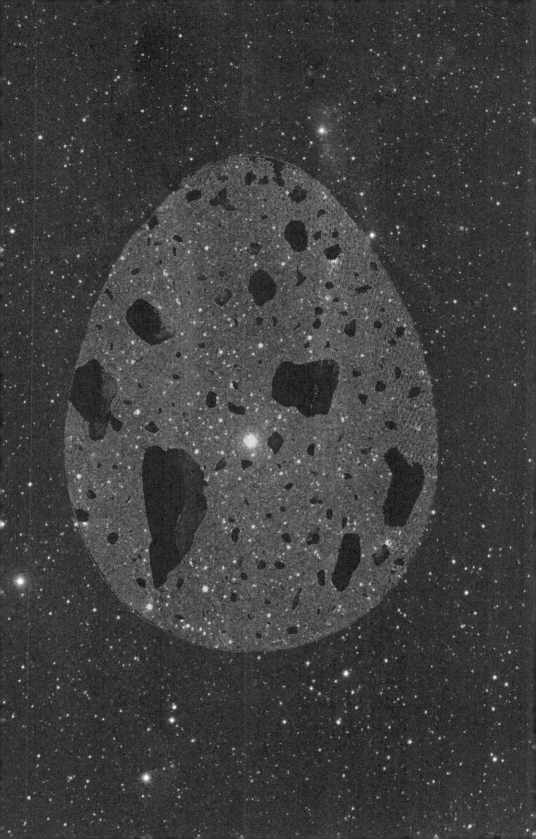

It seemed like I was in the grip of something inevitable. Grace's memory had everyone bound in invisible shackles. Was it possible she was somewhere inside of me? Or maybe she was outside of me, haunting me because she saw something of herself in me.

With everyone taking their posts, I had no choice but to walk through the door. As I lingered on the shoddy porch, Otto gave me some final words of advice.

"My mother was a kind woman, but she believed you should pay for your crimes. That man in there...he committed crimes. Against you. So keep that in mind. It isn't revenge. It isn't evil. It's justice, and you're the only one who can give it."

I realized what he wanted me to do with that gun.

"Justice? You think I'm going to shoot someone? There's no way!"

Otto held out one of his big hands to steady himself on the crumbling handrailing. "Then I don't know what. I don't know. We'll have to let God decide."

This family had obviously experienced some trauma, but I reminded myself that it wasn't my problem. Otto would just have to be disappointed. I wasn't going to kill some poor old man.

Seeing no point in any further conversation, I went on inside. If I failed the test quickly, maybe they'd take me back home that very night.

The old place was tidier than I would have expected. It was threadbare and had a sour smell, but there weren't any big holes in the floorboard or the ceiling.

In the first room, the old man had several wooden chairs and tables, all of them piled high with old books.

The sound of something clanking in the other room startled me.

"Hello?" I said, gripping my gun.

"Oh, hello!" A hoarse but friendly voice called out. "I'm just having some tea. Won't you join me?"

I stepped carefully in his direction and found him setting a kettle on an old pea green stove. His kitchen was dark except for the dim light in the range hood.

"I always add enough water for at least four cups. You never know how thirsty you'll be." He looked up at me, and his blue eyes sparkled like stars.

"Do you know who I am?" I said.

He gave me an 'aw shucks' smile. "I am forgetful these days. I reckon, though, that you're one of my dear church friends. You all never leave me lonely for long."

That deranged family had sent me to shoot an old man with dementia! I knew they'd all lost their minds, but this was beyond anything I'd ever heard of. Still, the old man made me feel a tad uncomfortable, so I couldn't talk myself into putting down my gun. Not yet.

"Thanks for having me," I said. My voice quivered a little, but I hoped he wouldn't notice.

"I always have lots of tea. Would you rather have lemon-ginger, or would you like regular black tea? I also have some spiced tea that the pastor's wife brought me. It's from a mix, but it's not sugar-free if that's important to you."

I almost asked for the spiced tea, but I remembered being drugged by Sandra, so I asked for the lemon-ginger in a pre-made bag. If I found myself getting sleepy, I'd run out the door and beg for Otto to take me away.

The kettle soon boiled, though, and I got my mug of lemon-ginger tea. He led me into his room full of stiff wooden furniture covered with books, and he cleared out a seat for me. I kept my hot mug in my lap since I saw nowhere to set it down.

"Have you been doing research?" I said. I looked at some of the books and saw that a lot of them had the words "Animal Husbandry" in the title.

"I breed animals. Well, I used to. I think they've all been sold now. But I like to keep up with it just in case. See, it's a science and an art. Choosing the best animal for the best animal. You have to see beyond their forms and into their souls."

He was a short guy with frizzy white hair standing up in all directions. His ratty-looking gray wool sweater probably gave him the staticky hairstyle, and he wore it with gray pants that looked like they'd once been black before being washed a million times and accumulating a layer of dust. He lived there all alone, though, so it didn't matter what he looked like. He probably wasn't looking for another wife.

"It's strange to see a woman hunting," he said. "Usually they aren't tough enough."

"Some women are good hunters, but the truth is, I'm not tough enough," I said.

Saying it out loud was some relief, but I also felt ashamed. Maybe it was my fault that I hadn't managed to toughen myself up in the early part of my life.

He gave me a sympathetic smile. "You're much too beautiful for a job like that. I could tell that such a beautiful girl wasn't suited for it."

The compliment warmed me. I couldn't help but appreciate his charm and his easy manners even though he didn't understand who I was or what was happening. We had that in common.

"Can I ask you a question about your wife?"

"Oh, yes. About Grace."

"You remember her? What happened to her?"

"God, yes. The terrible tragedy of my life. Grace was so unhappy. Do you know she threw herself out of the car while I was driving, and she did it twice? The first time, she only had a few scrapes, I think. But the second time, she got so banged up, she died a week later. She must have thought she'd be as lucky the second time as the first time. God rest her soul."

"I heard she got hurt so badly, she couldn't have any more children for some reason. Did that happen when she jumped out of the car?"

If I looked through the curtains just right, I could see Otto's sullen face bathed in moonlight. He was keeping watch outside the front door. I wondered if he could hear us.

"That's what she told people. But she wasn't really hurt that first time. God was protecting her."

"He wasn't protecting her the second time?"

I went to church, but theology didn't make much sense to me. If something went their way, people would say God blessed them. But when something bad happened, they said they couldn't understand why it had happened.

He winked at me. "You're a clever girl."

I might have blushed a little. "I just ask questions," I said.

"That's a great thing. Do you have any more questions for me?"

The old man seemed so safe, so kind. But in the twinkle of the inner young man's eyes, I thought I saw something dangerous. Maybe all young men are dangerous, and maybe it never quite goes away. I'd learned to always watch them. I'd had bad dates, just like anyone. I'd trusted men I shouldn't have trusted. I couldn't quite forgive myself for the times I'd been so eager to trust. I always told myself that nothing really bad had happened to me, and that was true in a way. But I was still angry about what had happened. I didn't get off scot-free.

"The truth is, your family thinks I'm your wife. Reincarnated. What do you think?" I said.

His eyebrows rose and fell. "You're a thousand times prettier than Grace ever was. Maybe a million. I knew Grace from the time she was seventeen. She had many good qualities. She was a hard worker. She was clean. She was a good cook. Unfortunately, she was also crazy. Not only are you beautiful, but you seem sane."

"I guess." Plenty of guys had called me crazy. "But what happened before Grace jumped out of the car? What made her do that?"

He shook his head like she was a hopeless case. "She got one of her paranoid notions. She always thought I had it out for her. I don't know where she got that idea. But her parents were crazy, too. They always thought someone was out to get them. Poisoning their well. They were always worried something would happen to one of the kids, that they'd be kidnapped or hurt. Wouldn't let them do anything."

"I was kidnapped," I said. "I never thought a thing like that could happen. I usually think of myself as lucky, but that only works if I forget the bad things that have happened to me. I used to think it was better to forget the bad things. But they keep coming back. Just this morning, my only sin was trying to help a lost kid, and I was kidnapped for it. Bad things aren't supposed to happen when you're doing a good deed."

"That sounds terrible," he said, shaking his head at the evils of the world. "I'm so sorry about that."

Of course, he didn't know what I was talking about, but unlike his son and his son's family, he knew how to be polite.

"I guess you don't talk to your son Otto anymore?"

"His mother poisoned him against me. But fortunately, my church family helps me. Do you have a church family?"

"Sort of," I said. My young professionals' group at church was mostly for networking and finding dates.

"I love mine. I recommend it. Much more loyal than my blood family. They help me keep the place clean. Help me buy groceries. Someone always comes to pick me up for Sunday service, too."

"That's great." I wondered if I would go help an old man down the street if I lived there. The people in the area didn't seem to have much money. Would I share some small amount I had with this man? He seemed nice enough. And yet, the longer I spent in his presence, the stranger I felt. When I was a kid, sometimes I'd eat too many butterscotch candies from my grandparents' candy bowl, and I'd feel sick and weak for about an hour. That's how the old man made me feel.

"What's your name?" he asked me. He was the first person in his family to ask. But the rest of them must have already known.

"Charlotte."

"You know what that means?"

"I was named after my father since he didn't have a son. It's a version of Charles."

"That's right. It means free man. You'd like to be free, wouldn't you?"

He gave me a look that pierced my heart.

"I would."

"Not just free from this place. Free indeed."

"What do you mean?"

I felt sort of woozy, and in that moment, I seemed to see from two sets of eyes. With one pair, I was in a dank old house with an old man. With another pair, I was falling from the passenger side of a car onto the cold road with a fire in my chest. I wondered if I was empathizing with Grace too much. After all, she was supposedly me. Up until that moment, though, I hadn't been empathizing with her at all. It was hard for me to see her as anything but a crackpot old lady who had caused me a lot of trouble.

He stared at me like he could tell what I was thinking. A threatening look was in his eyes, wasn't there? I couldn't tell for sure. I didn't know him, after all, and he had dementia. He might have been remembering something from the long gone past, forgetting entirely who I was.

"Mr. French?" I said.

"Who is that?"

I felt so sorry for him. He didn't even remember who he was. "It's your name, sir."

"My name is Abernathy."

"But your son is Otto, right? His last name is French."

If he were in my life, I'd have to explain things over and over. I imagined it would be tiring. I was already getting bored with the old man, in a way. I was starting to dislike him, though he hadn't done anything to hurt me. He'd only been kind to me.

"He took a different name then! Is he saying he's French? Damn him. I mean, what kind of silly, put-on show is that? You can't change who you are."

I wanted to argue with him, but I didn't have any facts. I thought people could change who they were. They could learn to stop giving into addictions, and they could move to a new country, and they could read a thousand books, and all those things would change them.

It dawned on me suddenly. He'd been able to hide his feelings for me at first. He'd pretended he thought I was a visitor from his church, but he knew who I was all along. He was looking at me like I was a strung-up animal, something he could eat when he was ready. He was still attracted to Grace, in spite of everything. And he still hated her. He didn't care what she looked like on the outside.

"You do think I'm her, don't you?" I was afraid of angering him, but I reminded myself that I was the one with the gun.

"I never bought into my late wife's weird star search. She thought she was a real prophet. I never knew any of her prophecies to come true."

"She found things in the stars to remind her of herself. So she'd remember when she came back," I said. I stood up, holding the gun tighter than I had before, and I looked out the window. The stars were so clear. I'd never really paid attention to them.

In a way, I wanted it all to be true, at least for that evening. Something was wrong with the old man, and something was wrong with his whole family. I was in HR, after all. I liked to solve people's problems. How could I walk away when there was such a big mess to clean up? I'd need better tools than that old worn broom or those eyeglasses with the wrong prescription. I didn't need glasses at all, in fact.

"Well, it's late for me. I reckon I'd better go to bed. There's a guest room where Otto's old room used to be if you want to use it. I can't remember if the sheets have been changed lately, but there are clean ones in the closet by the bathroom."

"You want me to stay?"

"Well, I can't exactly turn you out. Not with all the wolves out there." He gave me a wry look as he nodded at the front door. He must have known Otto and his family were out there. He must have felt their hatred for him.

"I'm not sleepy, but I'll make the bed if I need to."

"Sure thing. Hold on, let me get you something."

He plodded down the hallway, and when he returned, he tossed an old baby blue hat box onto the ground, and it exploded with costume jewelry that scattered all over the floor.

"This was Grace's, since you're so interested in Grace. You can have it if you want. No one else wants it. Cheap stuff, you know. I've tried offering it to the ladies at church, but they ain't interested."

He said it so sharply, like he was trying to cut me with his words. I only wore classic pieces, gold with small real gems. In recent months, I'd started to wear silver earrings because they were in, but they didn't suit my skin tone. I looked down at all the plaster beads, the purples and the reds and the glitter-filled and the flower-shaped. The stern-looking Grace in that picture didn't look like she wore this silly stuff. Maybe she saved it up and just looked at it, never trying it on.

And the smell of that box was so familiar. Citrus and musk. It didn't smell like the light floral perfume I wore. The smell got inside of me. I wanted it on my skin.

I looked up to ask him if she'd worn any of it, and which was her favorite piece, but he was already gone. I went to the hallway and saw that his door was closed and his light was dark. So quickly he'd put himself to bed.

What did I care what Grace did with her jewelry? But I got on my knees and picked up the scattered pieces, and I put them back in their special box. Once they were together again, I raked my fingers through the necklaces like I was exploring the contents of a pirate's chest. I was especially enamored of a gold chain with a plastic owl pendant. It seemed to mean something. And these could all be mine if I was willing to accept a gift from that old man. I tried to imagine myself wearing them to work. I looked down at my navy blazer that was covered in grease stains. Bright jewelry could be a nice feminine contrast to business attire. Since I was new at my job, I'd been playing it safe and wearing conservatives suits and crisp white shirts and neutral pumps. I still felt like I was playing dress up. But what if I did it forever? That is, for the rest of my life. I'd get tired of it and want to wear something colorful.

I wondered if Grace had worn the jewelry anywhere special. She was a housewife, and it sounded like she didn't get around much. According to the old man, she was in the passenger seat of the car when she jumped out. Twice. She must have felt like she was trapped. Kidnapped, in a way. Even if our personalities were different, our tastes, our experiences—maybe we'd had some of the same bad things happen to us.

As I was playing with the beads, I found a little brooch shaped like a snake and covered with the fakest and shiniest of spring green stones. I wondered if she adored snakes or if she hated them. It seemed to me that both adored and despised things might end up on a person's list of star shapes.

A snake. Like the Garden of Eden. He'd come in to mess things up between the man and woman. Satan in the snake's disguise.

I closed my eyes for a moment, and I could see a woman handing me a piece of chalk-white fruit. The fruit smelled rotten,

like the time some little creature crawled up in my air duct
and died. A corpse fruit. Her offering it to me. Some roles get
reversed. I wasn't always a woman, was I? Maybe I was the man
once, too, and maybe I was once the snake. If I was a snake in my
memory, could have been the woman offered fruit to me. Maybe
she was the one. Otto said that you keep coming back as your
own kind, but what did he know? Maybe you could come back as
an egg, a tomato, a squash, a pie, a snake, an ant, a dog, a broom,
a shovel, a frying pan, a needle, a camellia, ivy, a pine, a chair, a
quilt, a book, a cup, a hat, a ring, eyeglasses, a shotgun. Maybe I
had been all kinds of things until it was time to be something else.

But no proof of that. Just a crazy thought. Under the
influence of the madness of the days. I'd been had, been double-
crossed, been caught, been kept. I held my gun tighter.

You can't trust anyone. You can't. A man might come to
you and seem so sweet and handsome, so dapper and mature.
He might ask to marry you. He might bring you flowers. He might
hold your hand in the park in front of all the other girls. He might,
he might. No telling what he'd do when his front door was closed.
He could hate you for no reason, or for a reason he wouldn't give.
He could terrify you. He could tell you you were nothing. If you
can't trust a snake, then you can't trust a man, because every man
has been a snake in one of his lives. Some men have been crawling
on their bellies so long, it looks just like they're dancing.

He'd been rough with little Otto, too. No doubt. That must have been why Otto hated him so much he wanted to change his name. Was that why she'd jumped from the car those two times?

The first time when she wasn't hurt was a miracle. She must have believed she could do it a second time. But even the Son of God didn't get out of the world without dying. She plotted her star chart, her homemade map of the cosmos, and she did it when she was dying. When she was bleeding all inside of her body.

I could see it all so clearly, like a memory. Could have been my imagination, too. If someone tells you something enough times, you start to wonder. You can give yourself memories. But then, if you remember something, maybe you make it happen in the past. If we are like gods, if God made creation out of nothing, then maybe we can make things out of nothing, too. Maybe I could become Grace even if I'd never been her.

That was crazy, crazy. And the old man had said Grace was crazy. But just because something was crazy didn't mean it wasn't true.

And anyway, he had to pay for what he'd done. He'd hurt Grace. And Otto, his own little boy. He'd beaten them. He'd cussed them. He'd made them scared to be in their own home. I could see it in my mind, the bruises he gave them. The scrapes. The broken bones. I was sure of it. I remembered it like I remembered getting my first bike. Like I remembered my first kiss. The house brought it back to me. It had once been a cozy place, however humble. But he had filled it full of pain.

If he didn't die, there was no justice. After what he'd done, he'd lived such a comfortable, pleasant life. He'd made so many friends with his sickening charm, subtle like the snake. And she'd been duped into marrying him and letting him make her miserable for years and years.

If he died, it would be one less worry for the people at church. One less problem for Otto and Sandra and John and Seth. Who cared? He needed to die, at long last, for his crimes. He'd killed Grace. I was sure of it. He'd pushed her out the car. She hadn't jumped. When I closed my eyes, I felt his cold grip on my shoulder. I could feel myself pushed out onto the road.

Otto had grown and was strong by then. He never would have tried it while Otto was around. But Otto had to go to work sometime. I'd found him Sandra, and he was saving up to build them a house. Buy them some land. She was a special one. She had the special sight, though she didn't know it at first. Such a shy thing. So humble. With time and work, I knew one day she'd prophesy almost as well as me.

Sure, I knew I was going to die. And I wouldn't have needed a prophet to know it. He wanted me to die. He couldn't divorce me, or it would have hurt his good name. If all he'd done got out in court, if the gossip spread, he'd be an outcast in town. At church.

Why should I feel bad about bringing justice down? God might have sent me to do it. I plotted it out. I used a map of the stars I'd made, and made my calculations. I knew that girl was going to re-be me. I told it to Sandra. I told her what hospital, what time it would be. She found her for me.

If I didn't kill him, if I walked away and let myself live a different life, then I'd never forget it. I'd never forgive myself. I'd feel an itch in my heart the rest of my life. Some part of the past would remain.

I took the safety off the gun. I walked down the hall and knocked on the old man's door. Softly at first, like I was afraid to make him angry. Old habits.

"I want to talk to you!" I called out.

"Door's unlocked," he called back.

Maybe he was holding a gun at me. I had mine ready when I opened the door and flicked on the overhead light quite suddenly.

No. He was lying there, squinting in the harsh light with no weapon. A small frail human being.

"I'll give you one chance," I said. "Repent, and I'll spare you."

It felt so good to say it. Like Jesus coming down in a robe of light and glory, coming to judge the quick and the dead.

He sat up in bed. "Repent for what?"

The nerve of that man. I set my jaw. I cocked my gun.

"Repent for what you did to me and my son."

He let out one single laugh, and it sounded more like a scream. In some ways, he'd been terrified of me.

"You made that all up in your crazy mind," he said. "I never done nothing but support you. Make money for you. You got to thinking you were a prophet, honey. That's the kind of thing crazy people think. They think they're Napoleon or God or something."

"Plenty of people have been prophets," I said. "It's not like being God."

"Well, those prophets probably knew something. You didn't have anything in that head of yours. If you were such a great prophet, why didn't you tell Sandra her little girl was going to die? Why didn't you figure out where she was going to be born again so they could find her? John told me all about it, back when he still used to visit me. Now none of them come near here, like I have a plague."

"You do," I whispered. My heart seized up, and my hands started shaking. I wanted to aim the gun right, but I didn't know how. If I had once known how to shoot it, maybe the memory would guide me.

"You're no prophet. You're just a weird old woman. I don't think you reincarnated in this young thing. I think you've just possessed her, taken her over. You hang around this old house because you've got nowhere better to go, and you finally found a spot to land on. You've been haunting me so long. I knew you never went away. You'd never have the decency."

"You speak of what you do not know. I'm a prophet, not a ghost. But no prophet can foresee all things. I didn't know their child would die. That breaks my heart. But God didn't show me that.

All I know is, I'm Grace again. Right here. And I'm going to kill you for what you did."

But could I? Could I kill someone? Could I watch their face explode, watch them bleed? I didn't think so. I'd never been able to stand the sight of blood and gore. My hands were shaking and shaking. I was worried I'd miss.

"Shoot me then!" he roared at me. Like old times. He sat up taller in bed. "I've lived too long as it is. I lived far better once you were gone. And don't you dare, don't you dare come find me! If I get born again into another body, you leave me alone for the rest of time!"

I pulled the trigger, and then his arm was bleeding. A hit, but not in the right spot. He cried out in pain, a kind of helpless agony I'd never heard from him before. I almost pitied him, almost wanted to help him.

But I remembered all he done. This was the fruit of it. This was the crop he planted, and he had to reap it.

So I racked it, and I pulled the trigger again. And I did it again. And again. But my hands shook so bad. Otto ran in, and he had to finish the job, put the old man out of his misery.

His hands shook too. He started crying, blubbering some words I couldn't understand. Sandra came running in with an old shovel and handed it to me.

"Time to dig," she said.

4.

The shovel was my last shape. I just had to break the earth with it to complete the ceremony. Otto did some of the digging, though John did most of it.

After the shooting, Otto and I cried and carried on, but Sandra and John and Seth were cool as the midnight air. They burned the bloody sheets. We were far enough from any other house that no one would know what had happened. We buried him in the woods. Since he had dementia, folks from the church would figure he wandered away. The police wouldn't find his body, would think animals had eaten it. That's what Sandra said. I don't know if she's a prophet, but she's smart.

When I looked up at the stars through the trees, I spotted the egg in the sky first, and then the ant. I spun around and took in the twenty-two shapes of my old life, swirling all around me.

When the body was deep enough in the ground, we burned our bloody clothes and wore stuff the old man had in his closet.

I gathered up Grace's old costume jewelry. We went back home, and I took a bubble bath that turned red. I kept taking fresh baths until I came out clear. Then I went to bed.

I slept and slept. No dreams. Just rest.

A knock at the door woke me. For a desperate moment, I couldn't remember who or where I was.

"Lunchtime!" a little kid called out. Seth's voice. I felt almost fond of him.

I put on the old man's clothes again. With a belt, the pants stayed up. I kind of liked his old green sweater. Maybe I'd keep it as a kind of souvenir.

I went downstairs with a light heart, a spring in my step. I could hear birds squawking up overhead on their way south.

Sandra had made ham sandwiches for lunch with potato salad and black-eyed peas.

"I love potato salad," I said when I saw my plate, but I couldn't remember how long I'd loved it.

"I know," Sandra said, the biggest smile on her face.

Otto still seemed tired, and yet he was also at peace. I could see it in his easy ways. Something had snapped. Something had changed for the better.

The boys were laughing and joking with each other, stealing things from each other's plates. They weren't being polite, but I laughed at them. They were such healthy, strong children. If only the little girl hadn't gotten away from us. The poor thing.

"I'll pray," Sandra said. "Dear Lord, thank you for blessing us. Thank you for helping things finally go our way."

I was so hungry, I ate three plates like we were having Thanksgiving dinner. We didn't talk about what had happened. I didn't want to, and I guess neither did they.

When the meal was done, I helped clean up. Afterwards, we sat around the living room drinking coffee, and finally, I asked the one question that was bothering me. "What's going to happen to me now?"

I asked it to Sandra. She seemed to glow with inner wisdom. Something in her shy heart had changed.

"Well, you sure are Grace now. Not all the way, but last night she broke through. She spurted up in you like a wellspring. She's in your blood. I expect that if you look for her, you'll be full of her, but if you ignore her, she'll get quiet."

I'd felt her memories so vividly the night before, but already they were fading. I'd felt the utter urgency of killing that old man. But I thought about my old life, my family and friends and job. I was doing so well at work. I wanted a new boyfriend, and I had a couple of prospects. I wanted to be myself. But if she was really inside of me, how could I ever be myself without also being a little bit of Grace?

"I want my life as Charlotte back," I said. They were disappointed, but they understood.

"I expected it," Sandra said. "That's how rebirth works. Even someone like Grace, when put in a new body, wants to live a new life. It's for the best that we never found my sweet little Annie. She has a new life, too, now. I don't want to worry her and take it from her."

She'd been stone-faced at the killing, but now tears came to her eyes. I got up and hugged her.

"But I'm still sorry I couldn't find her for you. I'm sorry I never foresaw it."

These confessions and apologies and forgivenesses, they did us all some good.

On the drive back to Birmingham, I rode in the backseat instead of in the trunk. John and Seth stayed behind at the house, and I gave them both big hugs before I told them goodbye. The lock on the car door was still duct-taped, but Otto pulled it off to show he trusted me. I trusted them, too, in my way. I fell asleep on the ride.

It woke me when we got to the city and church bells were ringing out. Sunday morning. I felt giddy and strange as I hurried from their car to mine.

"Call us soon!" Sandra said.

Otto got choked up and couldn't talk.

I promised to call. I got into my car and raced back to my apartment, and once inside, I put the old man's clothes in my hamper and put on my pajamas. I figured I'd decide what to do with them later, whether to keep them or burn them or give them away. Instead of worrying about anything, I watched a show I'd been in the middle of, picking right up like nothing had happened. For the rest of the day, I felt the inner joy that comes from having done a good deed.

Maybe I was sick. I fell asleep early, around eight, and I woke up shivering in the middle of the night.

I flicked the light on, sure I'd find someone in the room with me. But I didn't even have a goldfish at my apartment. I lived there all alone.

There was no one there that I could see. When I got up to check the place, I found the locks still locked, and no one hiding under the bed or in any of the closets.

I put on my robe and stepped out on my balcony to breathe the fresh air. I couldn't see as many stars as I'd seen in the country. I couldn't make out the egg or anything, but I saw the Big Dipper.

"I'm losing her," I said to myself. As she slipped away and I felt like me again, it was hard to think of what I'd done. I'd shot an old man to pieces. Maybe he was a bad old man, but he'd been a stranger to me. Who was I? Would God have mercy on me?

I went back to bed and cried for myself. I wasn't what I was before. Whether I was Grace's reincarnation or not, I was also Charlotte. Yet I could feel Grace in the center of my chest like heartburn. I swallowed, and she went down little by little. The more she disappeared from my mind, though, the guiltier I felt. I hated guns. I'd never pulled a trigger in my life. That family had kidnapped me and made me a killer.

I couldn't tell the police on them, or I'd get in trouble, too. I had a secret, a shame I'd carry for the rest of my life. Maybe I wouldn't be marked on the outside like Cain was in the Bible, but I'd be marked on the inside. I'd always been so confident, so pretty, so clever. Now I'd second-guess myself. I'd be quieter. I knew that was going to happen. Was already happening.

Was it better to try to get my old life back? People could change, after all. Maybe I could forgive and forget myself.

I decided not to decide. The next morning, I might call in sick to work, or I might go in and say I was fine. I could do my work just like before. Work was one thing I had. It would distract me. Grace had been unlucky for the most part, and I couldn't let her take my luck away from me.

On future nights, I'd go out and try to find my own shapes in the stars, stuff like sea shells and mimosas. Things I liked. I deserved to find my own shapes in the sky, not to be plagued with eggs and ants and snakes and brooms. I begged the Grace inside me to go to away. It was my time. She had her chance. I'd done more for her than anyone could have asked.

Acknowledgments

Thanks to everyone perceiving this!

Thanks to my family and friends.

Thanks to Alana for her creepy/funny artwork and innovation.

Thanks to my parents and brothers for their encouragement.

Thanks to Robert Ottone and all friends of Spooky House.

Thanks to Brandi Wells, Caleb Stephens,
Christi Nogle, Kelsea Yu, and TJ Price. And thanks to other writers
I've met for their inspiration. I look forward to reading all the work
you produce in the coming years.

Thanks to Lady Bird, a wonderful beagle, whose spirit lives on.

Thanks to my husband for everything.

About the Author

Ivy Grimes is from Birmingham, Alabama, and someday she'll return. Visit her at www.ivyivyivyivy.com to read some short stories. Also, check out her little collection Grime Time from Tales From Between and the forthcoming collection Glass Stories from Grimscribe Press.

About the Illustrator

Alana Baldwin is from Birmingham, Alabama and holds an MFA in Book Arts from The University of Alabama, a BFA in Graphic Design from Auburn University and has spent the previous fifteen years working in various creative environments: academia, in-house, fine art and art production and agency. She co-operates a collaborative letterpress shop and small-edition book-bindery out of Northport, Alabama. Under the Open Letter Press (OLP) umbrella, Alana works with themes of cause and effect and seeks to reconnect audiences with the exploratory spirit of youth.

Also Available from Spooky House Press

Helicopter Parenting in the Age of Drone Warfare by Patrick Barb

The White Horse by Rebecca Harrison

Deeply Personal by Alexis Macaluso

Boarded Windows, Dead Leaves by Michael Jess Alexander

The Disappearance of Tom Nero by TJ Price

Her Infernal Name & Other Nightmares by Robert P. Ottone

Residents of Honeysuckle Cottage by Elizabeth Davidson

Her Teeth, Like Waves by Nikki R. Leigh

Coming Soon

Clairviolence Vols. 1 & 2 by Mo Moshaty

Printed in the USA
CPSIA information can be obtained
at www.ICGtesting.com
JSHW081203041123
51230JS00005B/184